Sheppard Homans

Report Exhibiting the Experience of the Mutual Life Insurance Company of New-York for Fifteen Years Ending February 1, 1858

SALZWASSER
VERLAG

Sheppard Homans

Report Exhibiting the Experience of the Mutual Life Insurance Company of New-York for Fifteen Years Ending February 1, 1858

Reprint of the original, first published in 1859.

1st Edition 2023 | ISBN: 978-3-37513-576-8

Verlag (Publisher): Salzwasser Verlag GmbH, Zeilweg 44, 60439 Frankfurt, Deutschland
Vertretungsberechtigt (Authorized to represent): E. Roepke, Zeilweg 44, 60439 Frankfurt, Deutschland
Druck (Print): Books on Demand GmbH, In de Tarpen 42, 22848 Norderstedt, Deutschland

REPORT

EXHIBITING THE EXPERIENCE

OF THE

MUTUAL LIFE INSURANCE COMPANY

OF

NEW-YORK,

FOR

FIFTEEN YEARS ENDING FEBRUARY FIRST, 1858.

PRINTED BY ORDER OF THE BOARD OF TRUSTEES.

NEW-YORK, NOVEMBER, 1859.

TABLE SHOWING THE PROGRESS OF THE COMPANY.

No. of Policies in force on the first of February in		Amount assured thereby.	Assets.	No. of Policies in force on the first of February in		Amount assured thereby.	Assets.
1844	462	1,611,718	$32,311 05	1852	6,512	16,406,865	$1,627,655 56
1845	971	....	97,471 36	1853	6,797	17,599,773	2,060,649 30
1846	1,856	....	216,980 28	1854	7,373	19,660,027	2,543,301 61
1847	2,616	....	325,005 31	1855	8,118	22,182,633	2,850,077 56
1848	3,620	....	551,575 27	1856	8,778	24,904,110	3,309,085 80
1849	4,473	12,457,769	758,473 14	1857	9,794	28,024,012	3,787,945 76
1850	5,799	14,969,481	1,000,439 62	1858	10,390	30,481,302	4,685,908 95
1851	6,242	15,666,476	1,298,388 46	1859	10,993	32,575,099	5,374,933 42

TO THE BOARD OF TRUSTEES.

GENTLEMEN :

In presenting the Financial and Mortuary Experience of this Company during the first fifteen years of its existence, as developed by the Actuary, I take occasion to state some facts connected with its history.

The first Actuary of this Company, the late CHARLES GILL, demonstrated its Experience upon a portion of its business to the period of its second dividend in 1853. (See his Reports of 1851 and 1853.)

These documents, marked by the general ability which distinguished his acts, embraced but a portion of the business of the Company, and though valuable as a commencement, yet their scope, both as to extent of observation and the subjects embraced, was necessarily too limited to fully meet our requirements.

Our present Actuary, Mr. HOMANS, from his advanced point of observation, has not only taken up, and brought down to the date of his statement, the line of facts contained in the former Report, but he has enlarged the basis of demonstration, developing facts of vital statistics obtained by the Company from other sources, at much labor and expense, as well as by the results of its own experience.

The intelligence and industry the Actuary has exhibited in the preparation of this Experience, and the clearness and skill with which he has demonstrated it in his tables and diagrams, will be apparent to you in examining the document now submitted. The importance of collecting vital statistics from all quarters where our business extends, can not be

overrated. Those collected by public authority in this country are mostly
unreliable from the incompetency or unfaithfulness with which they are
gathered and arranged. Those obtained from abroad, while more correct
in representing facts, are not only taken from too narrow a territorial basis
to suit our purposes, but belong to classes differing from ours in constitu-
tion, habits, and employments, nearly as much as the country they inhabit
does in geographical extent and position. Again, vital statistics as they
exist and are demonstrated in an entire community comprising both sexes, all
ages, employments, and conditions, throw little light upon the business of
Life Assurance. The classes who assure their lives are taken out from the
whole mass included in the census returns, and embrace mainly professional
men, merchants, manufacturers, and a few farmers and mechanics, from the
ages of 20 to 56.

Our observation and experience among those who have been Assured in
this Company already embrace a larger number of persons than those comprising the entire population from which the Carlisle and Northampton
Tables were formed, which Tables for a long period and until quite recently
were those mainly used by the Life Assurance Companies of Europe. Among
English Companies the " Equitable," one of the oldest and most successful,
was the first which contributed the results of its Mortuary Experience. It
derived its chief value from being the first attempt to ascertain the value
of *assured lives*. The next was the celebrated Actuaries' or Experience
Table, which embraces results from the records of seventeen different Life
Companies, namely, Equitable, Amicable, Alliance, British Commercial,
Crown, Economic, Guardian, Imperial, Law, London, Norwich Union, Pro-
moter, Royal Exchange, Scottish Widows' Fund, Sun, Universal, and the
University. The Equitable, Amicable, Eagle, and very recently the Economic, have separately investigated and made public the results of their
experience.

In the United States, the Report of the Experience of this Company made by the late Mr. GILL, was the first attempt, as already stated, although on a somewhat limited scale, to ascertain the value of assured lives in this country. The "Mutual Benefit," of New-Jersey, have in their Annual Reports for 1857 and 1858, published the probable and actual number of deaths in their Company, from which various tables contained in the present Report have been computed by our Actuary with as much accuracy as the limited facts stated would admit.

Our own experience, though more favorable than the Actuaries' Table, or that of any other known, both in its pecuniary results and in its relative mortality, compares more nearly to the Actuaries' than to the Carlisle or Northampton Tables.*

On assuming my present official duties, and seeing the great importance of American vital statistics and an American experience in Life Assurance, I applied to other Companies to join with us in gathering from public sources and from such local agents and examining physicians in different sections of the country as could be reached, such facts as might be useful to all.

I regret to say that I had not a single response to this appeal from any Company, and that the facts gathered and arranged by Dr. WYNNE on our appointment, and published as a "Report on Vital Statistics," and distributed to our Trustees, and others, were from data exclusively collected and furnished by ourselves.

During the past two years another attempt has been made to obtain the experience of different Companies not only in their general results, but

---

* For our favorable mortality experience the Institution is much indebted to the skillful and thorough examinations of Dr. POST, our Medical Examiner, who in 1853 and in 1858 prepared the Mortuary Reports of the Company. Dr. Post is now engaged in bringing the Reports in a classified form to this date, and when finished, it will be published in a future edition of this work.

with special reference to Term Policies, proffering our own experience in return, but, as in the former case, without any response in the form of a report, unless the instance already alluded to, forms an exception.

It is hoped that neither apathy among officers, want of ability on the part of the mathematicians employed, nor a disinclination to compare results, have led to inaction in a matter of so much importance to all.

The Marine Underwriter who would venture to insure vessels to navigate the ocean and our inland waters without furnishing himself with proper local charts and the results of experience in the risks that he covers, would scarcely display more imprudence than our Life Assurance Companies do by a blind reliance on an experience three thousand miles distant.

With almost equal prudence and security might he take the Ordnance Survey of the Coast of Great Britain, and assume that it represented the depth of water and currents of our coast and harbors, as we to venture to predicate entirely the cost and results of Life Assurance over our broad country with all its variety of climate, races, habits, and occupations, on the results of that isolated district with its even climate and homogeneous races.

Impressed with these views, we have for several years watched the development of the experience of this Company with unceasing scrutiny and solicitude, and under the authority of the Board have from time to time made such changes in the Rates and in the Policies issued, as to conform both to a sound and equitable standard.

The result at the present time is thus described by the Insurance Committee in their recent Report:

"They congratulate the Trustees that the Report demonstrates the Company to have been so managed as to present the best experience in its vital statistics, as well as in its pecuniary results, ever attained in the same period by any similar Institution. It appears that the Officers of the Company have been so fully aware of the facts of this experience as they have been developed in its business and (under the authority of the Board) to have made such proper arrangements and modifications in the extra rates required of residents in various classes and of different conditions, where practicable, as to render any further alterations for the present unnecessary. The facts of our experience fully justify all the changes made in the past four years, both as to Term Policies and to the additional rates charged for certain classes of risks."

The Board have determined that the Report of Experience, which was printed for the *private use* of the Trustees, shall now be gratuitously given to the public for their benefit, in the hope that this example may be followed by other American Companies.

The future growth and magnitude of Life Assurance in this country, may be conjectured from its past progress.

No people are more capable of understanding its advantages than ours, and by none will they be more cordially and extensively embraced; but they will require to know that the Companies they join are based upon sound principles and are pursuing a sound policy.

The fundamental principles of Life Assurance are few and simple, resting upon the ascertained duration of human life, a proper selection in the lives assured, and a sufficient rate of premium to cover the risk taken, if invested at a rate of interest certain to be realized. Beyond this, in the practical application of these principles, a competent amount of scientific attainment, of knowledge of the races of men, their physical constitutions, habits, and occupations; the diversities of climates, and the prevailing diseases incident to each, and of the actual cost of the several extra risks to be taken is necessary, and this knowledge should be settled and applied by a wise and discriminating judgment.

As no Company in this country will claim to possess, in its Executive management, all these qualifications, with a requisite duration and extent of experience, to verify its proceedings, all must see the great importance of combined wisdom and united action if the business of Life Assurance is to occupy the commanding eminence here to which it is entitled.

The Actuary's Report of Experience made to the Board of Trustees in November last, is as follows.

I am, very respectfully,

Your obedient servant,

F. S. WINSTON,

NEW-YORK, Nov. 15, 1858.   *President.*

ACTUARY'S REPORT.

GENTLEMEN:

·The close of the third quinquennial period since the formation of this Company, embracing nearly half a generation, seems an appropriate time for making a careful examination of the results of its Experience in respect to the mortality amongst members; as well to ascertain in what particular circumstances of class, term, or age, we have been successful or otherwise, as to indicate what modifications, if any, should be made in our present practice. For these reasons I have continued the observations commenced by the late·Mr. GILL, from which results of Experience might be deduced; with special reference to the determination of the comparative mortality among members residing in the different classes; among holders of short term and whole life policies; and also of the relative mortality at different ages or epochs of life.

It may perhaps be well to remark that this Company assures at the age according to the " nearest birthday," assuming that the errors of deficiency and excess will balance each other. This is different from the practice of English Companies, who assure at the age "next birthday," which has the effect of representing their members to be older than they are in reality, (about four months on the average.) With the exception of this single assumption, that the *office age* is the *real age*, the results which are now presented are deduced from the most rigorous calculation. The number of *lives* exposed to mortality are carefully separated from the number of *policies*, and no care or labor has been spared in making the various observations and deductions as complete and accurate as possible. The annual Experience of the whole Company has been noted separately, for each of the fifteen years ending February 1st, 1858, as may be seen by reference to the following Table.

TABLE I.

Annual Experience of the whole Company—1843-57 inclusive.

Year.	Exposed to Mortality in the Company for one whole year.		Probable Loss by Company's Table.		Actual Loss.		Probable Loss by Carlisle Table.	
	No. of Lives and fractions of Lives.	Amount.	No. of Deaths.	Amount.	No. of Deaths.	Amount.	No. of Deaths.	Amount.
1843	253.59	966,716	2.962	11,461			2.809	10,902
1844	633.79	2,312,278	7.715	29,703	5	18,000	7.297	27,119
1845	1,275.15	4,346,769	15.539	54,518	7	18,100	14.771	51,626
1846	1,993.53	6,226,630	24.934	80,436	23	69,400	23.528	75,809
1847	2,656.14	8,128,045	33.550	106,741	28	66,150	31.733	100,392
1848	3,505.38	10,707,618	44.155	140,014	27	94,200	41.798	131,983
1849	4,513.43	13,290,200	56.551	173,986	64	175,950	53.491	163,859
1850	5,297.94	15,127,795	67.320	200,261	71	154,640	63.613	188,391
1851	5,572.93	15,867,144	72.181	213,790	49	164,100	67.970	200,296
1852	5,730.17	16,713,162	76.277	228,051	67	203,100	71.649	213,924
1853	6,131.07	18,508,266	83.315	257,197	72	207,200	78.019	239,581
1854	6,720.07	20,723,856	92.127	289,339	85	281,500	85.864	269,294
1855	7,250.76	22,870,264	100.506	321,332	81	267,850	93.653	298,490
1856	8,185.60	26,148,107	113.374	367,014	75	264,255	105.599	340,985
1857	8,898.24	29,121,868	123.876	408,790	96	328,100	115.195	379,813
Total,	68,617.79	211,059,018	914.377	2,882,633	750	2,312,545	856.989	2,692,464

These results are deduced from observations embracing every variety of age, term, and climate, which constitute the Company, as a whole. The comparison is therefore not strictly just, inasmuch as we should expect that the mortality among members residing in the South or California, and who pay an extra premium, would prove to be greater than that obtaining among members residing in the New-England or Middle States, who are insured at the regular table rates. Each class, term, and age, however, will be considered separately in the sequel.

It may be well here to state the reason why the second column of this table contains the number of lives and *fractions* of lives exposed to mortality for one whole year. It is found more convenient, in computing the Mortality Experience for any given year, to assume *one year* as the unit, rather than *one life;* instead of saying, for instance, that we have *one life* exposed to mortality for *one third* of *a year*, we find it more convenient to say that we have *one third* of *a life* (.33) exposed to mortality for *one whole year:* the results in each case being precisely the same. By repeating this process for each life in the office, we have the *exact* number of lives and *fractions* of lives exposed to mortality for *one whole year*. Out of this number living we may readily determine the number which should die during a given year, according to any table of mortality. In this manner the Experience has been determined separately, for each year of the Company's history, and the results are believed to be quite as favorable as were ever attained by any Life Company in the world. They afford satisfactory proof that the predictions by our theoretical Table of Mortality have, so far at least, been more than sufficient to cover losses actually sustained. It is only by thus carefully noting the *annual* Experience, and after the lapse of a sufficient number of years *combining* their results, that information, at once practical and reliable, can be obtained. We have now had fifteen years' Experience, the combined results of which for every age may be seen by the following table:

TABLE II.

GENERAL EXPERIENCE OF THE MUTUAL LIFE INSURANCE COMPANY OF NEW-YORK, FOR FIFTEEN YEARS, ENDING FEBRUARY 1ST, 1858.

Age.	Exposed to Mortality in the Company for one whole year.		Probable Loss by Company's Table.		Actual Loss.		Probable Loss by Carlisle Table.		Amount of act. Losses.
	No. of Lives and fractions of Lives.	Amount.	No. of Deaths.	Amount.	No. of Deaths.	Amount.	No. of Deaths.	Amount.	
14	22.10	$60,562	0.132	$362			0.118	$335	
15	38.52	74,746	.237	460			.239	463	
16	42.01	69,176	.266	438			.280	464	
17	54.58	97,349	.356	634			.376	673	
18	61.60	91,711	.413	615			.427	639	
19	109.45	183,025	.755	1,263	4	6,000	.758	1,283	
20	172.90	298,087	1.228	2,117	1	600	1.219	2,105	.58%
21	271.68	554,732	1.986	3,963	4	7,100	1.848	3,853	1.97
22	396.32	819,659	2.982	6,168	5	10,000	2.771	5,733	1.36
23	596.83	1,207,574	4.619	9,345	4	4,000	4.204	8,505	.67
24	806.13	1,674,654	6.415	13,327	10	16,300	5.716	11,878	1.24
25	1,046.36	2,290,504	8.562	18,743	11	14,500	7.653	16,753	1.05
26	1,290.30	3,028,871	10.855	25,482	11	26,000	9.507	22,317	.85
27	1,589.81	4,097,960	13.755	35,455	8	29,750	12.350	31,833	.50
28	1,877.73	4,937,100	16.716	43,950	11	22,350	16.328	42,948	.50
29	2,069.02	5,604,777	18.948	51,329	20	33,500	20.324	55,084	.966
30	2,312.85	6,400,502	21.799	60,325	26	82,000	23.356	64,664	1.124
31	2,503.43	7,139,038	24.281	69,242	21	55,800	25.527	72,861	839
32	2,700.65	7,850,626	26.961	78,373	31	86,100	27.354	79,527	1.147
33	2,811.82	8,362,402	28.894	85,932	26	57,100	28.260	84,050	.924
34	2,994.62	9,092,211	31.683	96,196	35	79,350	30.404	92,313	1.17
35	3,020.93	9,288,660	32.907	101,181	29	76,500	30.985	95,274	.90
36	3,049.80	9,486,108	34.210	106,406	35	91,800	32.075	100,098	1.15 1.15
37	3,067.96	9,633,974	35.441	111,292	23	72,600	33.195	104,577	.75
38	3,049.61	9,690,711	36.290	115,320	30	108,500	34.055	108,216	.95
39	2,967.64	9,510,563	36.392	116,628	31	113,500	35.245	112,957	1.05
40	2,842.58	9,252,250	35.963	116,967	13	41,750	37.050	120,325	.44
41	2,686.54	8,823,127	35.033	115,054	21	69,050	37.005	121,539	.78
42	2,551.34	8,418,212	34.338	113,301	21	82,100	36.671	120,994	.73
43	2,407.72	7,981,164	33.477	110,970	28	85,800	35.110	116,381	1.163
44	2,254.94	7,506,844	32.417	107,918	23	75,000	33.368	111,086	1.010
45	2,077.77	6,981,958	30.919	103,898	21	75,400	30.776	103,396	1.011
46	1,899.11	6,481,796	29.322	100,079	15	43,500	28.135	96,034	.790
47	1,695.42	5,746,111	27.298	92,518	20	61,650	24.757	83,910	1.180
48	1,534.69	5,240,157	25.852	88,270	23	66,350	21.383	73,022	1.498
49	1,404.73	4,811,853	24.796	84,939	18	47,000	19.219	65,841	1.281
50	1,243.14	4,284,821	23.021	79,346	15	53,000	16.681	57,494	.804
51	1,090.47	3,779,253	21.198	73,465	17	97,000	15.583	54,013	1.557
52	949.08	3,279,651	19.379	66,967	12	40,000	14.427	49,854	1.264
53	822.56	2,863,411	17.656	61,463	15	46,000	13.283	46,238	1.822

TABLE II.—*Continued.*

Age.	Exposed to Mortality in the Company for one whole year.		Probable Loss by Company's Table.		Actual Loss.		Probable Loss by Carlisle Table.	
	No. of Lives and fractions of Lives.	Amount.	No. of Deaths.	Amount.	No. of Deaths.	Amount.	No. of Deaths.	Amount.
54	726.99	$2,501,514	16.424	$56,514	16	$65,600	12.283	$42,266
55	621.81	2,133,839	14.804	50,805	12	43,000	11.144	38,245
56	543.42	1,902,216	13.659	47,814	13	62,895	10.324	36,142
57	448.37	1,573,554	11.925	41,850	9	45,900	9.371	32,883
58	370.62	1,294,064	10.453	36,498	6	28,800	8.973	31,324
59	311.74	1,024,472	9.346	30,714	3	5,000	8.690	28,966
60	259.19	815,740	8.281	26,062	7	38,300	8.681	27,318
61	212.50	637,865	7.252	21,767	12	31,800	7.634	22,826
62	167.33	520,138	6.113	19,002	5	22,000	6.260	19,457
63	131.62	382,571	5.157	14,989	9	22,500	5.034	14,633
64	104.84	312,201	4.412	13,138	5	17,800	4.170	12,416
65	86.16	243,415	3.899	11,014	5	11,200	3.539	10,001
66	67.19	189,335	3.271	9,216	3	15,000	2.856	8,047
67	49.66	150,676	2.601	7,891	1	1,000	2.193	6,688
68	35.00	104,008	1.972	5,859	1	10,000	1.625	4,831
69	26.98	89,634	1.633	5,424	1	5,000	1.325	4,402
70	20.07	66,245	1.303	4,302	1	4,000	0.979	3,421
71	12.56	37,652	.881	2,642		....	.749	2,216
72	11.55	24,604	.876	1,865	1	1,000	.787	1,676
73	6.71	16,895	.549	1,383		....	.525	1,320
74	6.95	14,722	.615	1,302	1	2,000	.626	1,327
75	4.09	9,933	.391	949		....	.389	949
76	3.96	8,953	.409	924		....	.408	922
77	2.71	6,827	.302	761		....	.290	734
78	1.03	2,055	.124	247	1	2,000	.224	224
Total,	68,617.79	211,059,018	914.377	2,882,633	750	2,312,545	857.101	2,692,764

In order to give a clearer idea of the results contained in this Table, I have plotted in the following Diagram (No. 1) the numbers for each age, contained in the columns headed " Probable number of deaths," and "Actual number." Diagram No. 2 contains in a similar manner, a comparison of the " Probable" and " Actual" amount of loss, at each age. By means of these Diagrams the entire results of Experience may be seen at a glance.

I have also computed Tables, similar to the above, showing the Experience among members residing in each of the classes separately, in order to determine the comparative mortality among *assured* lives in different parts of the country. These classes are the same as those contained in the map prefacing the Annual Report for 1858, and explained in pp. 66–69. (See Report.) It will be observed that among the members of this Company are residents in all parts of the United States; hence the influence of almost every variety of soil and climate is exerted upon the lives and health of our assured, and renders the task of adjusting their varied interests one not only of great interest, but also of some difficulty.

It has not been thought necessary to present these different tables in detail, as the results contained in them may be observed by the following recapitulations:

TABLE III.

COMPARATIVE MORTALITY IN THE DIFFERENT CLASSES.

	Number of Lives and Fractions of Lives which have been exposed to the risk of mortality for one whole year.	COMPANY'S TABLE. Probable number of Deaths.	Actual No. of Deaths.	Per centage of Actual on Probable No. of Deaths.	Rate per cent of Actual Mortality.	Rate per cent of Probable Mortality.	COMPANY'S TABLE. Probable amount of Loss.	Actual amount of Loss.	Actual Loss to each $100 predicted.
Whole Company, 1843–52	31,432.05	401,166	340	84.75	1.08	1.28	1,238,944	963,140	77.74
1853–57	37,185.74	513,211	410	79.88	1.10	1.38	1,643,689	1,349,405	82.09
15 years	68,617.79	914,377	750	82.02	1.09	1.33	2,882,633	2,312,545	8J.22
Class I., 1843–52	19,937.20	255,088	178	69.78	0.89	1.28	......	......	....
1853–57	26,639.49	368,741	262	71.05	0.98	1.39	1,118,976	782,005	69.89
15 years	46,576.69	623,824	440	70.53	0.96	1.34	......	......	....
Class II., (including VI.) 1843–52	4,479.40	56,643	48	84.74	1.07	1.26	......	......	....
1853–57	6,393.45	85,012	79	92.93	1.23	1.33	264,428	230,650	87.22
15 years	10,872.85	141,655	127	89.66	1.17	1.30	......	......	....
Class III., 1843–52	1,569.50	20,199	20	99.01	1.27	1.29	......	......	....
1853–57	1,555.20	22,678	21	92.60	1.35	1.46	102,921	101,800	98.91
15 years	3,124.70	42,877	41	95.62	1.31	1.37	......	......	....
Class IV., 1843–52	1,441.10	18,575	23	123.82	1.24	1.29	......	......	....
1853–57	1,637.55	23,937	35	146.22	2.14	1.46	119,209	208,500	174.90
15 years	3,078.65	42,512	58	136.43	1.88	1.38	......	......	....
Classes V. & VII., 1843–52	861.10	8,837	37	418.68	4.30	1.03	......	......	....
1853–57	960.05	12,843	13	101.22	1.35	1.34	38,140	26,450	69.35
15 years	1,821.15	21,680	50	230.62	2.75	1.19	......	......	....

Nᵒ 1.

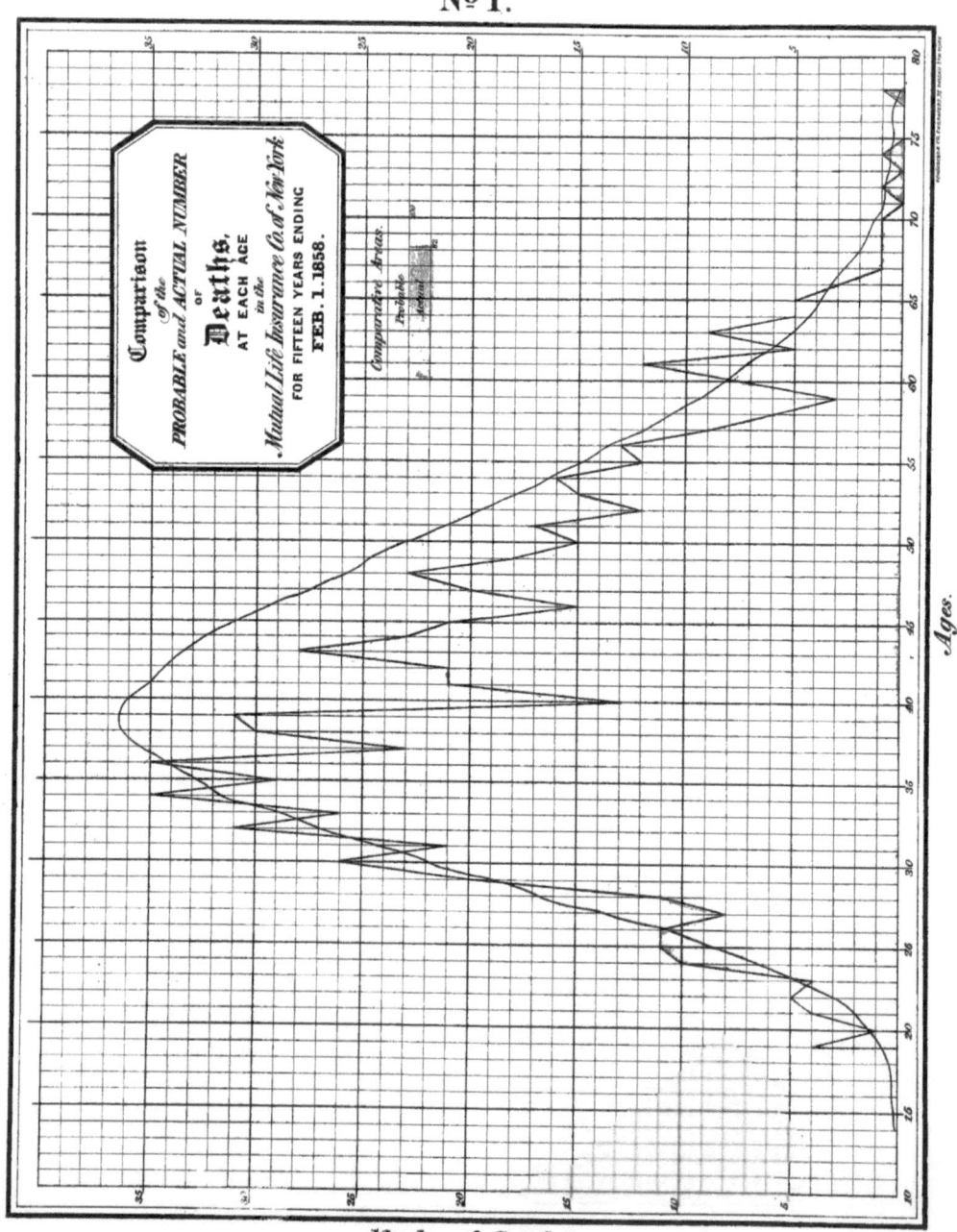

Comparison
of the
PROBABLE and ACTUAL NUMBER
OF
Deaths,
AT EACH AGE
in the
Mutual Life Insurance Co. of New-York
FOR FIFTEEN YEARS ENDING
FEB. 1. 1858.

Comparative Areas:

Number of Deaths.

Ages.

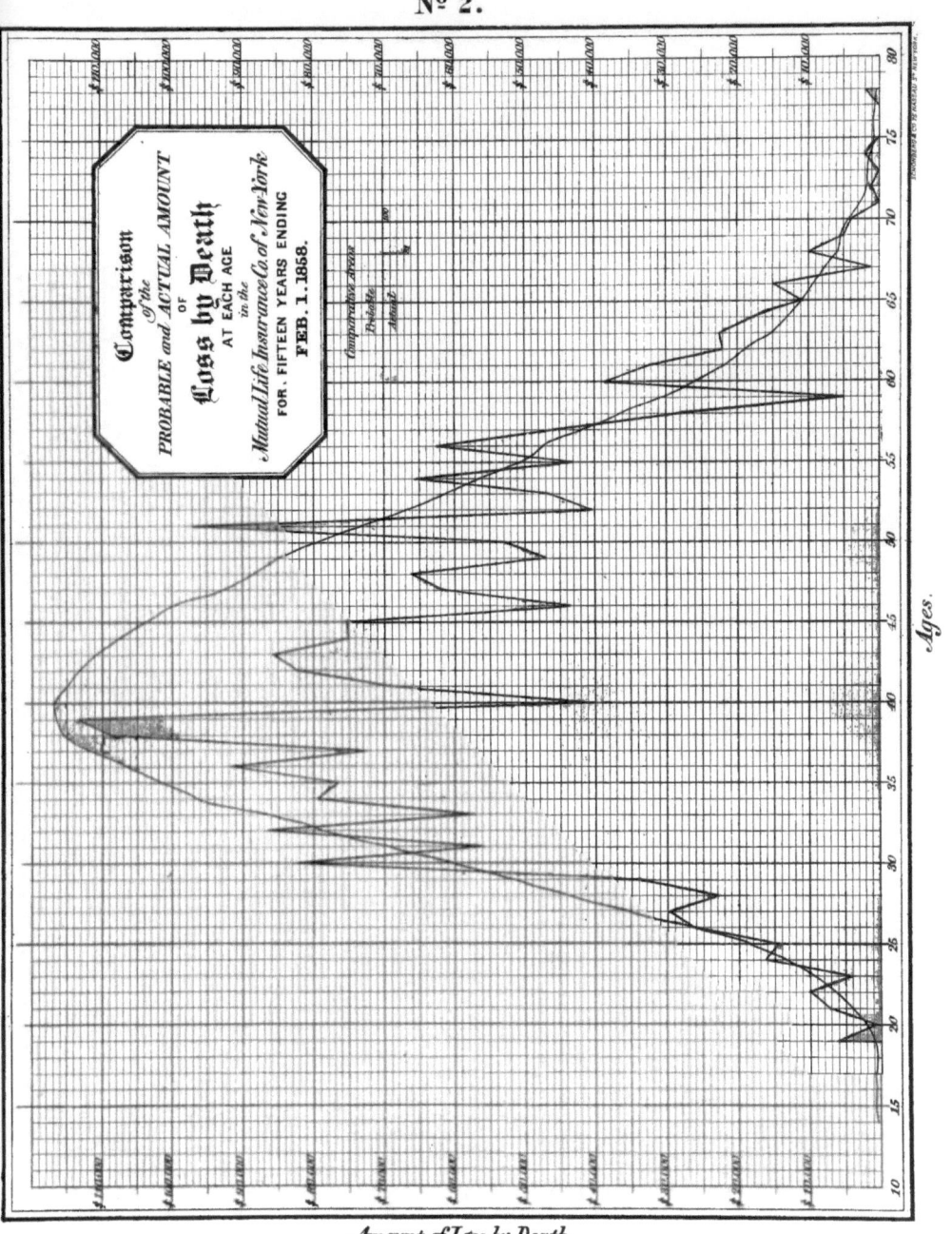

Comparison of the PROBABLE and ACTUAL AMOUNT OF **Loss by Death** AT EACH AGE in the Mutual Life Insurance Co. of New-York FOR FIFTEEN YEARS ENDING FEB. 1. 1858.

Amount of Loss by Death.

Ages.

We observe by this table of recapitulations the following comparisons, which of course include all ages:

1st. The entire results of Experience not only for the whole Company, but also for each class separately, during the first ten years, the last five years, and the whole fifteen years of its existence.

2d. The number of lives exposed to mortality for one whole year in the whole Company, with the corresponding numbers in each of the classes, during each period.

3d. The probable number of deaths according to the Company's Table of Mortality, in the whole Company, and in each of the classes separately.

4th. The actual number of deaths corresponding.

5th. The per centage of actual number of deaths on probable, or in other words the *actual* number of deaths corresponding to each one hundred *predicted* by the Company's Table of Mortality.

6th. The rate per cent of *actual* mortality which may be also read, by taking all the figures, as the actual number of annual deaths in the Company, out of each *ten thousand* lives exposed to mortality, both in the whole Company and in each of the classes separately.

7th. The rate per cent of *probable* mortality according to the predictions by the Company's Table, corresponding to the above.

8th. The probable amount of loss by the Company's Table, in the whole Company and in each class separately. I regret not being able to give a comparison of the actual and probable amount of loss for the first ten years in each class, on account of the want of time.

9th. The actual amount of loss in each class.

10th. The per centage of actual loss on the probable amount, or in other words, the actual amount of loss corresponding to each $100 predicted.

By means of these comparisons we may readily see that our best Experience has been in the New-England and Middle States, or near the Home Office, and that to a very great extent. That in Class II. or the Western States, in which residents are assured at regular table rates of premium, the Experience has not been quite so favorable, although within the predictions by our tables. We also observe that the comparative mortality among members residing in this class has materially increased during the past five years. It is true that these results include residents in Class VI., (in the immediate valley of the Mississippi,) in which an extra premium is charged, but by reference to the Report on the Experience among residents of St. Louis, (see "Minutes" Board of Trustees, February, 1857,) of which Class VI. is mainly composed, it will be seen that the mortality in Class II. proper, is very nearly as great as that in Class VI. alone.

We also observe that the mortality in Class III., or Southern States bordering on the Atlantic, has been more favorable during the last five years than in the first ten, and also slightly more favorable even than in Class II. One thing, however, should be borne in mind, that from the comparative scantiness of the data in this and in the succeeding classes, the results are not so reliable as those contained in Classes I. and II.

The mortality among members residing in Class IV., or the Southern States bordering on the Gulf of Mexico, has materially increased during the last five years, and to an extent somewhat alarming. The amount of loss, too, in this Class has been much larger than that anticipated.

Perhaps the most curious results of the above recapitulations are those referring to residents in California, (Class V.,) showing, for instance, that, while the actual number of deaths corresponding to each hundred predicted was, previous to 1853, nearly *four hundred and nineteen*, (418.68,) it was during the past five years, one hundred and one (101.22) only, owing no doubt to the increased facilities of procuring the comforts and necessaries of life in that State.

In order to give a clearer idea of the practical value of the foregoing results, I have arranged the following Table, in which columns A, B, and C, show the annual rate per cent of actual mortality among residents in each of the classes, for the first ten, the last five, and the whole fifteen years, respectively, according to the Experience of the Company. Column D shows the extra annual premium (per cent on amount of insurance) which should be charged for residence in each class, in order to place them all upon an equal footing, as far as regards the risk of mortality with Class I. alone. Column E shows in a similar manner the extra annual premium which should be charged in each class when compared with Classes I. and II. *combined*. Column F shows the extra annual premium now charged by this Company for residence in each class, in addition to the regular table rates.

TABLE IV.

	Annual Rate per cent of Mortality.			Extra Annual Premium which should be charged in order to equalize the risk		ExtraAnnual Premium now charged, per cent on Amount of Insurance.
	1843–52.	1853–57.	15 years.	with Class I. Per cent.	with Classes I. and II. Per cent.	
	A	B	C	D	E	F
Whole Company, ...	1.08	1.10	1.09	. . . .	. . . .	. . . .
Class I., ...	.89	.98	.96	. . . .	. . . .	. . . .
" II., ...	1.07	1.23	1.17	0.745	. . . .	. . . .
" III., ...	1.27	1.35	1.31	1.147	0.975	0.500
" IV., ...	1.24	2.14	1.88	2.867	2.634	2.000
" V., ...	4.30	1.35	2.75	5.449	5.158	1.000
" " since 1853, ...	. . . .	1.35	. . . .	1.290	1.092	1.000

These results, from the comparatively small amount of data, can scarcely be depended upon as furnishing reliable statistics of actual mortality in different parts of our country, and among all classes and ages; at the same time, however, they are believed to afford a more reliable comparison of the relative mortality among *assured lives* in the different classes than were ever before obtained. They prove conclusively that the extra rates of premium now charged by the Company, are not only judicious, but that they are in no case quite sufficient to provide for the extra risk which they are intended to cover, and consequently can neither be rescinded nor reduced, without doing injustice to members residing in the New-England or Middle States.

COMPARATIVE MORTALITY AMONG MEMBERS ASSURED UNDER SHORT-TERM AND WHOLE-LIFE POLICIES.

In order to throw some additional light upon this interesting question, I have computed the following Table, embracing results for the last five years only:

TABLE V.

Term of Policy.	Number of Lives exposed to Mortality.	Probable No. of Deaths Company's Table.	Actual No. of Deaths.	No. of Deaths to each 100 predicted.	Actual Rate of Mortality.	Probable Rate of Mortality.	Extra Annual Premium which should be charged.
Life,.........	33,222.52	460.56	341	74	1.02	1.39	....
Endowment,....	83.02	0.88	0	0	0.00	1.60	....
Seven Years, ...	3,255.56	44.03	56	127	1.72	1.35	1.090
Other short terms,	624.64	7.74	13	168	2.08	1.24	1.878
Whole Company,	37,185.74	513.21	410	80	1.10	1.38	....

The mortality among persons insured by short-term policies in this Company, has been found to be in all cases *inversely proportionate* to the *length of term* of the policy itself. Our Mortuary Experience among members assured under short-term policies is thus shown to have been very unfortunate, so much so, that by reference to the last column, we find that an extra annual premium of from *one* to nearly *two* per cent should be charged; which, added to the regular table rates, will make the gross annual premium on short-term policies nearly, if not quite as high as the *regular life rates*. In other words, Experience teaches that short-term policies should not be issued by this Company at less than life rates, thus practically confirming the wisdom and justice of the recent Resolution by the Board of Trustees, declining to underwrite these risks, at least until more reliable data than were then possessed could be obtained.

Applications for assurance under short-term policies, as was remarked by the President in his last Annual Address, are often made by persons who wish to provide for an extra hazardous risk, either of climate, occupation, or disease, *known only to themselves*, and in which the applicant has every advantage over the Medical Examiner; or they are made for the purpose of affording security for debt, both of which cases include contingencies not foreseen when naming the premium.

In the earlier practice of Insurance, when a life not altogether *first class*, was offered, the risk was sometimes accepted for a *short term* of years, and at a *small annual premium*, when it would have been rejected for the *whole term of life*, and at a *higher rate of annual premium*. I mention this singular fallacy to show that the science as well as practice of Life Insurance is progressive, and that the results of Experience furnish the safest and surest rules of guidance.

The following Table shows the exact number of Life, Term, and Endowment Assurance Policies, which were in force February 1st, 1858, with their corresponding *dividends* or *additions*, payable in all cases at death or with the policy itself.

TABLE VI.

Year of Issue.	Policies in force Feb. 1st, 1858.		Dividends or Additions to Policies in force.			
	No.	Amount.	1848.	1853.	1858.	Total.
1843	144	$482,300	$50,130 19	$43,959 38	$48,639 28	$142,728 85
44	198	656,750	57,388 91	60,564 84	66,935 62	184,889 37
45	378	1,025,950	66,217 67	94,561 49	106,727 82	267,506 98
46	398	969,030	42,837 75	92,986 76	102,891 69	238,716 20
47	585	1,599,115	36,058 65	158,595 03	173,598 21	368,251 89
48	535	1,396,773	3,277 00	120,467 25	152,018 54	275,762 79
49	652	1,608,300	2,337 18	110,653 15	178,428 76	291,419 09
50	537	1,252,600	7,539 93	68,916 01	143,290 32	219,746 26
51	400	971,244	2,954 85	32,274 24	110,720 84	145,947 93
52	476	1,388,600	2,932 62	17,984 09	161,788 08	182,704 79
53	620	1,823,827	....	5,744 50	195,660 76	201,405 26
54	866	2,634,237	....	8,281 06	220,185 07	228,466 13
55	1,018	3,472,660	....	6,124 67	209,800 71	215,925 38
56	1,297	3,874,010	....	4,083 19	148,285 58	152,368 77
57	1,372	4,342,850	....	1,272 26	58,785 72	60,057 98
Joint Lives,	9	35,100	28 46	1,276 16	2,073 15	3,377 77
Total Life,	9,485	$27,533,346	$271,703 21	$827,742 08	$2,079,830 15	$3,179,275 44

SEVEN YEARS.

Year of Issue.	No.	Amount.	1848.	1853.	1858.	Total.
1851	48	$127,400	$450 01	$1,502 39	$3,996 62	$5,949 02
52	71	198,400	1,388 23	1,980 96	6,919 26	10,288 45
53	65	217,300	....	2,867 75	6,311 72	9,179 47
54	83	262,650	....	1,986 96	5,424 26	7,411 22
55	104	320,550	....	1,314 37	5,955 87	7,270 24
56	106	339,000	....	1,381 32	4,675 60	6,056 92
57	95	274,000	....	...	758 21	758 21
Total,	572	$1,739,300	$1,838 24	$11,033 75	$34,041 54	$46,913 53

TABLE VI.—*Continued.*

Year of Issue, and Term of Policy.	Policies in Force Feb. 1st, 1858.		Dividends or Additions to Policies in Force.			
	No.	Amount.	1848.	1853.	1858.	Total.
Brought over,	10,057	$29,272,646	$273,541 45	$838,775 83	$2,113,871 69	$3,226,188 97

OTHER SHORT TERMS.

Year of Issue, and Term of Policy.	No.	Amount.	1848.	1853.	1858.	Total.
14 years,	1	$1,000	....	$36 07	$72 50	$108 57
11 "	1	10,000	....	86 83	507 02	593 85
10 "	14	79,000	....	988 52	2,281 54	3,270 06
9 "	1	10,000	....	....	....	....
8 "	1	4,000	....	....	93 27	93 27
5 "	106	305,550	....	43 34	2,774 14	2,817 48
4 "	1	200	....	....	....	....
3 "	8	26,600	....	....	180 83	180 83
2 "	20	88,200	....	....	611 29	611 29
1 "	21	66,700	....	....	169 55	169 55
Total,	174	$591,250		$1,154 76	$6,920 14	$7,844 90

ENDOWMENT-ASSURANCES.

Year of Issue, and Term of Policy.	No.	Amount.	1848.	1853.	1858.	Total.
Death or 40,	1	$2,000	....	....	$41 15	$41 15
" 45,	31	143,000	....	....	2,694 93	2,694 93
" 50,	53	180,000	....	....	4,226 91	4,226 91
" 55,	36	154,000	....	....	3,726 35	3,726 35
" 60,	34	125,800	....	....	3,562 65	3,562 65
" 65,	1	5,000	....	....	364 71	364 71
Total,	156	$609,800			$14,616 70	$14,616 70

POST-MORTEM DIVIDENDS.

Year of Issue, and Term of Policy.	No.	Amount.	1848.	1853.	1858.	Total.
Deaths, 1853	....	....	....	....	$1,894 56	$1,894 56
" 54	....	....	....	....	4,934 97	4,934 97
" 55	....	....	....	....	7,081 59	7,081 59
" 56	....	....	....	....	8,480 28	8,480 28
" 57	....	....	....	....	11,188 33	11,188 33
Total,	....	....	....	....	$33,579 73	$33,579 73
Total Office,	10,387	$30,473,696	$273,541 45	$839,930 59	$2,168,758 26	$3,282,230 30

COMPARATIVE MORTALITY AT DIFFERENT AGES.

In order to facilitate the interesting comparison of the relative value of life at different ages, I have computed the following Table No. VII., which is an "Adjusted Rate of Mortality according to the General Experience of the Mutual Life Insurance Company of New-York, for the fifteen years ending February 1st, 1858.

TABLE VII.

ADJUSTED TABLE OF MORTALITY ACCORDING TO THE EXPERIENCE OF THE WHOLE COMPANY FOR 15 YEARS ENDING FEBRUARY 1ST, 1858.

Age.	No. living.	No. dying	Rate per cent of Annual Mortality		Number out of which one Person will die annually.		Expectation of Life		Age.
			By Co.'s Experience.	By Co.'s Table.	Company's Experience.	Company's Table.	By Co.'s Experience.	By Co.'s Table.	
10	100,000	741	0.741	0.526	135.00	190.0	49.24	47.51	10
11	99,259	739	.744	.544	134.35	183.7	48.60	46.76	11
12	98,520	738	.749	.562	133.50	177.9	47.96	46.01	12
13	97,782	737	.754	.580	132.70	172.5	47.23	45.27	13
14	97,045	736	.758	.598	131.85	167.4	46.68	44.53	14
15	96,309	735	.763	.615	131.03	162.5	46.03	43.79	15
16	95,574	734	.768	.633	130.20	157.9	45.38	43.06	16
17	94,840	733	.773	.652	129.35	153.5	44.73	42.33	17
18	94,107	732	.778	.671	128.50	149.1	44.07	41.60	18
19	93,375	731	.783	.690	127.68	144.9	43.41	40.88	19
20	92,644	732	.790	.710	126.60	140.8	42.75	40.16	20
21	91,912	732	.796	.731	125.57	136.8	42.09	39.45	21
22	91,180	733	.804	.753	124.45	132.9	41.42	38.74	22
23	90,447	733	.811	.774	123.35	129.2	40.75	38.03	23
24	89,714	734	.818	.796	122.24	125.6	40.08	37.32	24
25	88,980	735	.826	.818	121.11	122.2	39.41	36.61	25
26	88,245	735	.833	.841	119.98	118.9	38.73	35.91	26
27	87,510	736	.841	.865	118.86	115.6	38.05	35.21	27
28	86,774	737	.849	.890	117.74	112.3	37.37	34.51	28
29	86,037	738	.857	.916	116.63	109.2	36.69	33.82	29
30	85,299	738	.866	.943	115.53	106.1	36.00	33.13	30
31	84,561	739	.874	.970	114.44	103.1	35.31	32.44	31
32	83,822	739	.882	.998	113.35	100.2	34.62	31.75	32
33	83,083	740	.891	1.028	112.29	97.3	33.92	31.07	33
34	82,343	740	.899	1.058	111.25	94.5	33.22	30.38	34
35	81,603	740	.907	1.089	110.24	91.8	32.52	29.70	35
36	80,863	740	.915	1.122	109.34	89.1	31.81	29.03	36

TABLE VII.—*Continued.*

Age.	No. living.	No. dying.	Rate per cent of Annual Mortality		Number out of which one Person will die annually.		Expectation of Life		Age.
			By Co.'s Experience.	By Co.'s Table.	Company's Experience.	Company's Table.	By Co.'s Experience.	By Co.'s Table.	
37	80,123	738	.921	1.155	108.53	86.6	31.10	28.35	37
38	79,385	736	.927	1.190	107.88	84.0	30.39	27.67	38
39	78,649	732	.931	1.226	107.47	81.5	29.67	27.00	39
40	77,917	726	.932	1.264	107.25	79.1	28.94	26.33	40
41	77,191	721	.934	1.304	107.03	76.7	28.21	25.66	41
42	76,470	717	.938	1.346	106.61	74.3	27.47	24.99	42
43	75,753	719	.949	1.390	105.37	71.9	26.72	24.33	43
44	75,034	729	.972	1.438	102.93	69.5	25.97	23.66	44
45	74,305	750	1.010	1.488	99.03	67.2	25.23	23.00	45
46	73,555	784	1.066	1.544	93.84	64.8	24.48	22.34	46
47	72,771	824	1.133	1.610	88.29	62.1	23.73	21.68	47
48	71,947	867	1.205	1.685	83.02	59.4	23.00	21.03	48
49	71,080	908	1.277	1.765	78.32	56.6	22.27	20.38	49
50	70,172	941	1.341	1.852	74.56	54.0	21.56	19.74	50
51	69,231	966	1.395	1.944	71.68	51.4	20.84	19.10	51
52	68,265	990	1.451	2.042	68.92	49.0	20.13	18.47	52
53	67,275	1,018	1.513	2.146	66.09	46.6	19.42	17.84	53
54	66,257	1,049	1.583	2.259	63.16	44.3	18.71	17.22	54
55	65,208	1,086	1.666	2.381	60.02	42.0	18.00	16.61	55
56	64,122	1,131	1.764	2.514	56.68	39.8	17.30	16.00	56
57	62,991	1,185	1.881	2.660	53.17	37.6	16.60	15.40	57
58	61,806	1,247	2.017	2.820	49.57	35.5	15.91	14.81	58
59	60,559	1,317	2.175	2.998	45.97	33.4	15.23	14.23	59
60	59,242	1,399	2.361	3.195	42.35	31.3	14.55	13.65	60
61	57,843	1,485	2.568	3.413	38.94	29.3	13.89	13.08	61
62	56,358	1,578	2.800	3.653	35.72	27.4	13.25	12.53	62
63	54,780	1,675	3.057	3.918	32.71	25.5	12.61	11.98	63
64	53,105	1,774	3.340	4.208	29.94	23.8	12.00	11.45	64
65	51,331	1,878	3.659	4.525	27.33	22.1	11.39	10.93	65
66	49,453	1,978	4.000	4.868	25.00	20.5	10.81	10.43	66
67	47,475	2,082	4.386	5.237	22.80	19.1	10.24	9.94	67
68	45,393	2,193	4.831	5.633	20.70	17.7	9.69	9.46	68
69	43,200	2,304	5.333	6.052	18.75	16.5	9.15	8.99	69
70	40,896	2,427	5.935	6.494	16.85	15.4	8.64	8.54	70
71	38,469	2,539	6.601	7.016	15.15	14.3	8.15	8.10	71
72	35,930	2,623	7.299	7.581	13.70	13.2	7.70	7.67	72
73	33,307	2,730	8.197	8.188	12.20	12.2	7.26	7.26	73
74	30,577	2,705	8.847	8.847	11.30	11.3	6.86	6.86	74
79	17,669	2,298	....	13.006	....	7.7	5.09	5.09	79
84	7,732	1,466	....	18.968	....	5.3	3.63	3.63	84
89	2,156	630	....	29.238	....	3.4	2.35	2.35	89
94	213	110	....	51.630	....	1.9	1.28	1.28	94
99	1	1	100.000	100.000	....	1.0	.50	.50	99

Some of the corresponding numbers from the Company's theoretical Table are also given, by means of which the "Annual Rate of Mortality," the "Number out of which one person may be expected to die in each year," and the "Expectation of Life," as determined by the results of our own Experience, may be readily compared, at each age, with the same num bers according to that Table. It will be observed that these numbers for both tables are the same after reaching the age of 70, which is owing to the fact that the number of lives exposed to mortality above that age in the Company, has been too small to furnish results at all satisfactory.

The relative mortality at different ages among members of this Company and also of the "Mutual Benefit," which we have deduced from data furnished in their last Annual Report, may be observed by Table VIII.

TABLE VIII.

COMPARISON OF THE *ACTUAL* NUMBER OF DEATHS CORRESPONDING TO EACH ONE HUNDRED *PREDICTED*, OR PERCENTAGE OF THE ACTUAL NUMBER ON PROBABLE, AT DECENNIAL AGES.

	15-25.	25-35.	35-45.	45-55.	55-65.	65-75.	All ages.
Class I. alone, ...	90	77	61	66	98	71	70.53
Class I. and II. combined,.	90	86	65	67	95	83	74.07
Class II. including VI.,.	89	127	80	71	83	195	89.66
Class III. alone, ...	662	85	96	90	99	0	95.62
Class IV. alone, ...	595	215	156	79	44	122	136.43
Class V. including VII., ...	431	337	159	201	0	0	230.62
Whole Company, ...	145	99	73	73	89	80	82.02
Whole Co., "Carlisle Table,". . .	157	99	74	88	101	92	87.52
"Mut. Benefit," " " . . .	191	101	80	84	72	103	87.62

Nᵒ 3.

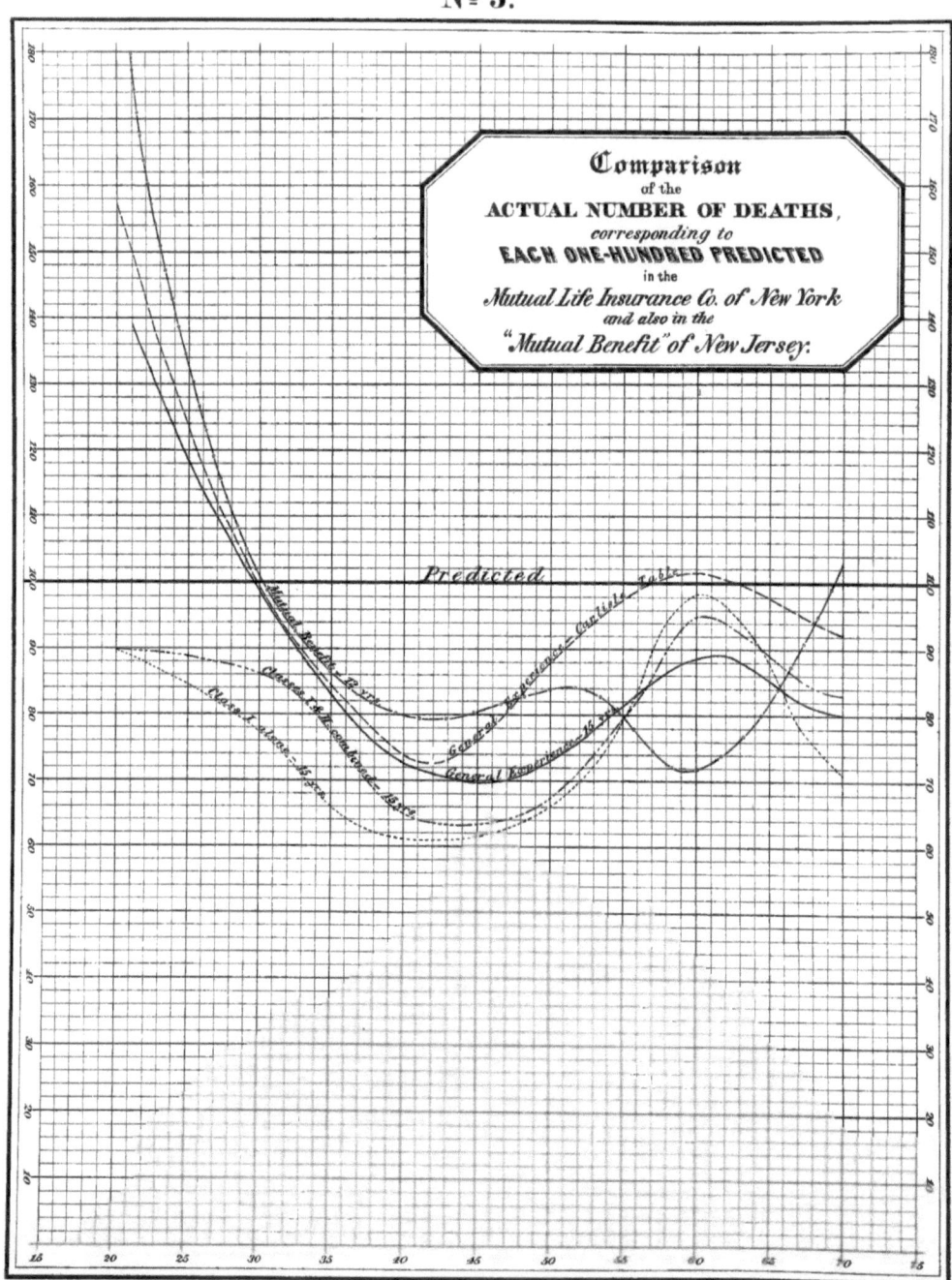

Comparison
of the
ACTUAL NUMBER OF DEATHS,
corresponding to
EACH ONE-HUNDRED PREDICTED
in the
Mutual Life Insurance Co. of New York
and also in the
"Mutual Benefit" of New Jersey.

Predicted

Mutual Benefit — 13 yrs.

General Life experience — Carlisle Table

Classes 5 & 6 combined — 13 yrs.

Classes 1, 2, 3, 4 — 15 yrs.

General Experience — 15 yrs.

Ages.

We first observe the extraordinary mortality at younger ages in the South and California, while in Class I. alone, as well as that in Classes I. and II. *combined*, it is in all cases less than that called for by the Company's Table. Some of these results are plotted in the accompanying diagram No. 3, by reference to which the comparisons may be more readily made. The horizontal line marked 100, refers to the predicted number of deaths, while the curved lines mark the actual number *corresponding* at decennial ages. We thus see how very large the per centage of actual deaths has been at young ages, and how small comparatively between the ages of thirty and sixty, after which the actual and probable results seem to approximate very nearly to each other, both according to our own Experience and that of the "Mutual Benefit," in a remarkable manner. One thing must still be borne in mind, however, that from the scantiness of the data, at very young or old ages, the corresponding results are not entitled to the same degree of confidence as those for intervening ages.

I have plotted in Diagram No. 4, the "Number out of which one person may be expected to die" each year, not only from the foregoing Tables, but also according to some of the more celebrated and reliable English Life Tables. The numbers at the bottom of this diagram represent the various ages from 15 to 75, or of the younger and older lives insured, while those on the side of the diagram represent the numbers out of which one person may be expected to die annually. In order to find the number according to any life table, we must note the points of intersection of the curve corresponding, with the horizontal lines, at each age. For instance, at the age of 20, we find that our curve of General Experience intersects the horizontal lines between the numbers *one hundred and twenty-six* and *one hundred and twenty-seven*, (126.60,) which means that out of every one hundred and twenty-six persons living at the age of 20, *one will die each year*, according to our own Experience. Our theoretical curve at the same age intersects the horizontal lines between the numbers *one hundred and forty* and *one hundred and forty-one*, (140.8,) which means that according to Mr. Gill's Table, we will have but one death annually out of every one hundred and forty-one persons living at the age of 20. At the age of 40, according to the same Table, one death will occur annually out of each seventy-nine persons (79.1) living, while it has been found by the General Experience of this Company, that we will have but one death annually out of every hundred and seven (107.25) persons living at that age. By thus noting for each age, the number out of which one person will die, according to any Table of Mortality, and then connecting the various points, we are enabled to determine the curve corresponding to the given table.

By an examination of the same diagram we may also observe the very great comparative value of life between the ages of 30 and 60, while below the age of 30, and particularly below that of 25, this value rapidly becomes less than we had anticipated from any previous observations. The excessive mortality at younger ages is perhaps owing to the fact that in this country young men are induced, by a spirit of enterprise, to enter upon the anxieties and cares of active business life too early. Besides, permanent habits of life and character are rarely formed below the age of twenty-five; while the effects of neglected education, bad habits, or ungovernable passions, then begin to manifest themselves, and all serve to render the risks on very young lives less desirable than those of somewhat older ages.

By comparing the different curves we may ascertain more clearly than by any other method, the peculiar *type* of our own curve of General Experience. We also observe that this curve approaches more nearly to the "Actuaries" than to our own, or to that of any English Life Table, unless it

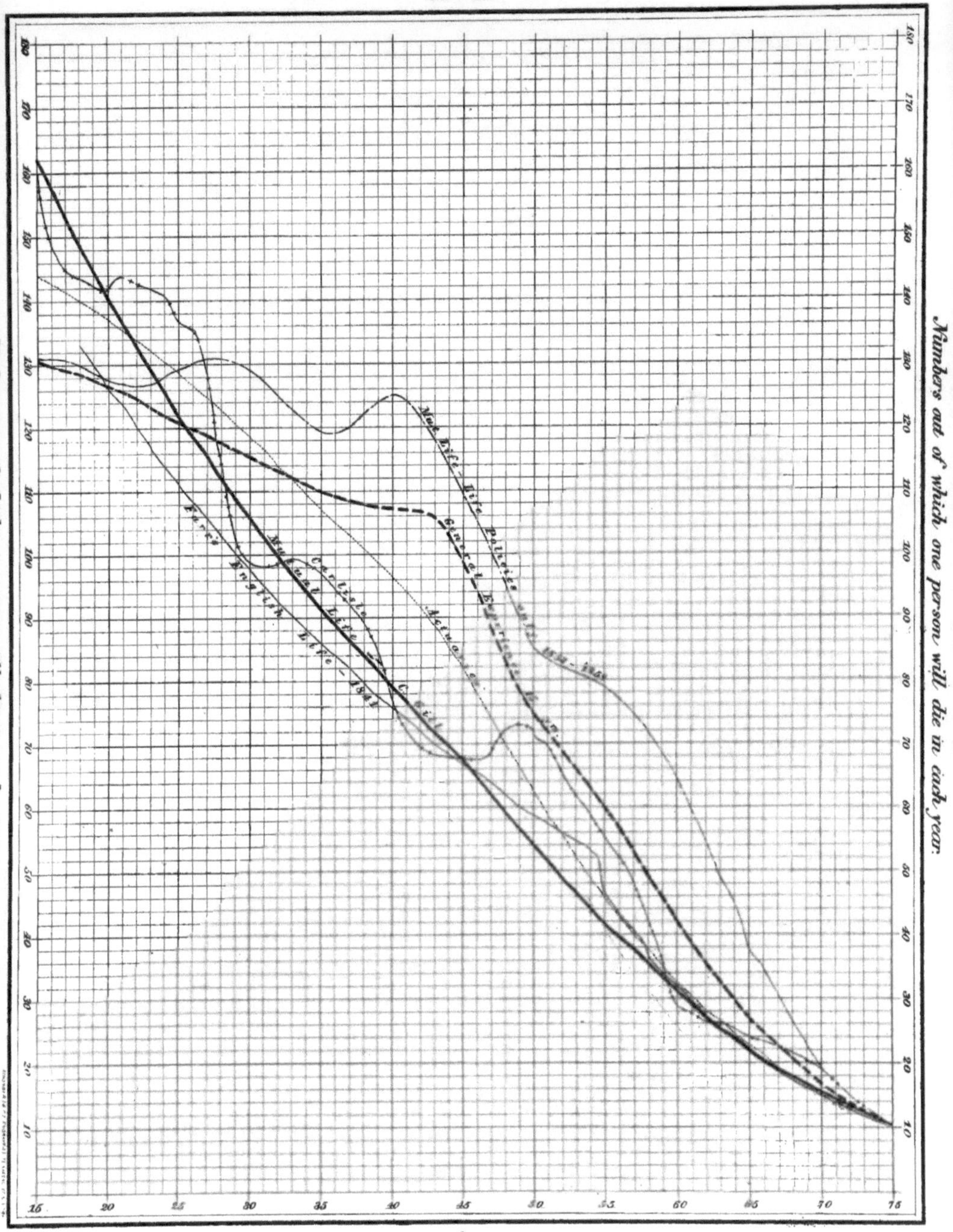

Numbers out of which one person will die in each year.

Ages.

No. Eng. Life

Carlisle

Mutual Life

Mutual English Life - 1841

New English Life

Actuaries

Ages.

be that of the Experience among members of "Friendly Societies," according to Ratcliffe, Neison, or Finlaison.*

By reference to the following diagram, No. 5, showing the number out of which one person will die according to the *unadjusted* Experience among members residing in Classes I. and II. *combined*, we find in the comparative *security of life* at different ages, the apparent anomaly of *two points* of *maxima* and two of *minima*, namely, at ages 27 and 42 for maxima, and at 24 and 34 for minima. In other words, the *value of life* or *chance of living during the ensuing year*, *increases* from the age of 24 to 27, *decreases* from this latter age to that of 34; again rapidly *increases* from the age of 34 to that of 42, after which the value again rapidly decreases, and with considerable regularity to the close of life.

I cannot think that this *anomaly* is entirely owing to the scantiness of the data from which our Experience was deduced. The same peculiarity was first noted by Mr. Finlaison, in his Report on the Mortality

---

* The annual rate of mortality among members of Friendly Societies between the ages of 16 and 75, and also among the members of this Company between the same ages, may be seen by the following Table.

	No. of Lives.	Deaths.	Annual Rate of Mortality
Friendly Societies, Ratcliffe, ...	621,472	6,049	0.9733
Do. Neison, ...	1,135,522	13,563	1.1944
Do. Finlaison, . . .	3,930,613	48,621	1.2370
Mut. Life, General Experience,	68,606	749	1.0917
Do. Class I. alone, ...	46,555	438	.9408

An Actuary in England once remarked, that the rate of mortality stated to prevail among members of Friendly Societies, was almost the same as saying that the working classes were immortal! But we find that the rate of mortality among members of this Company residing in Class I. is less than that by either of the above observations, which are based upon persons selected from among the *élite* of the working classes, and who were supposed to have the lowest rate of mortality known.

observed among Government male annuitants, published in 1829. He found, among males, that the point of greatest security in life was about the age of 13—*decreasing* afterwards to the age of 23, then *increasing* to the age of 34, after which it decreased, but so slowly, that at the age of 48, the value of life, or *chance* of living during the *ensuing* year, was somewhat *greater* than at the age of 23; after the age of 48 the value rapidly decreased until the close of life. These results were somewhat confirmed by M. Quetelet, from observations made in the kingdom of Belgium. And also by Mr. Neison in his valuable "Contributions to Vital Statistics," who found that this peculiarity occurred among members of "Friendly Societies," and *varied* with *different occupations*. Thus among agricultural laborers the value of life is greater at the age of 30 than at 23. Among country workmen, *not laborers*, the value is less at the age of 19 than at 25, and *again* less at 30 than at the age of 32—somewhat similar to our own experience. Among clerks there are also, in the value of life, two points of maxima, namely, ages 35 and 47, and two of minima, 28 and 44; while among bakers there are *three* points of each, namely, ages 22, 38, and 54 for the maxima, and ages 18, 31, and 49 for the minima. I also find (from data furnished in their last Annual Report) that the Experience of the "Mutual Benefit" shows the same anomalies, as may be seen by reference to the diagram No. 5, having, in the value of life among their assured, two points of maxima, namely, ages 31 and 40, and two points of minima, namely, ages 21 and 36.

Such anomalies are not observed when the observations are made among miscellaneous communities of men, women, and children, but seem to be peculiar to certain classes of persons, and no doubt similar facts, at different ages, might be deduced from observations among *female* lives alone. Various explanations have been offered by such men as Quetelet, Prof. Buchanan, etc., but which would be out of place here.

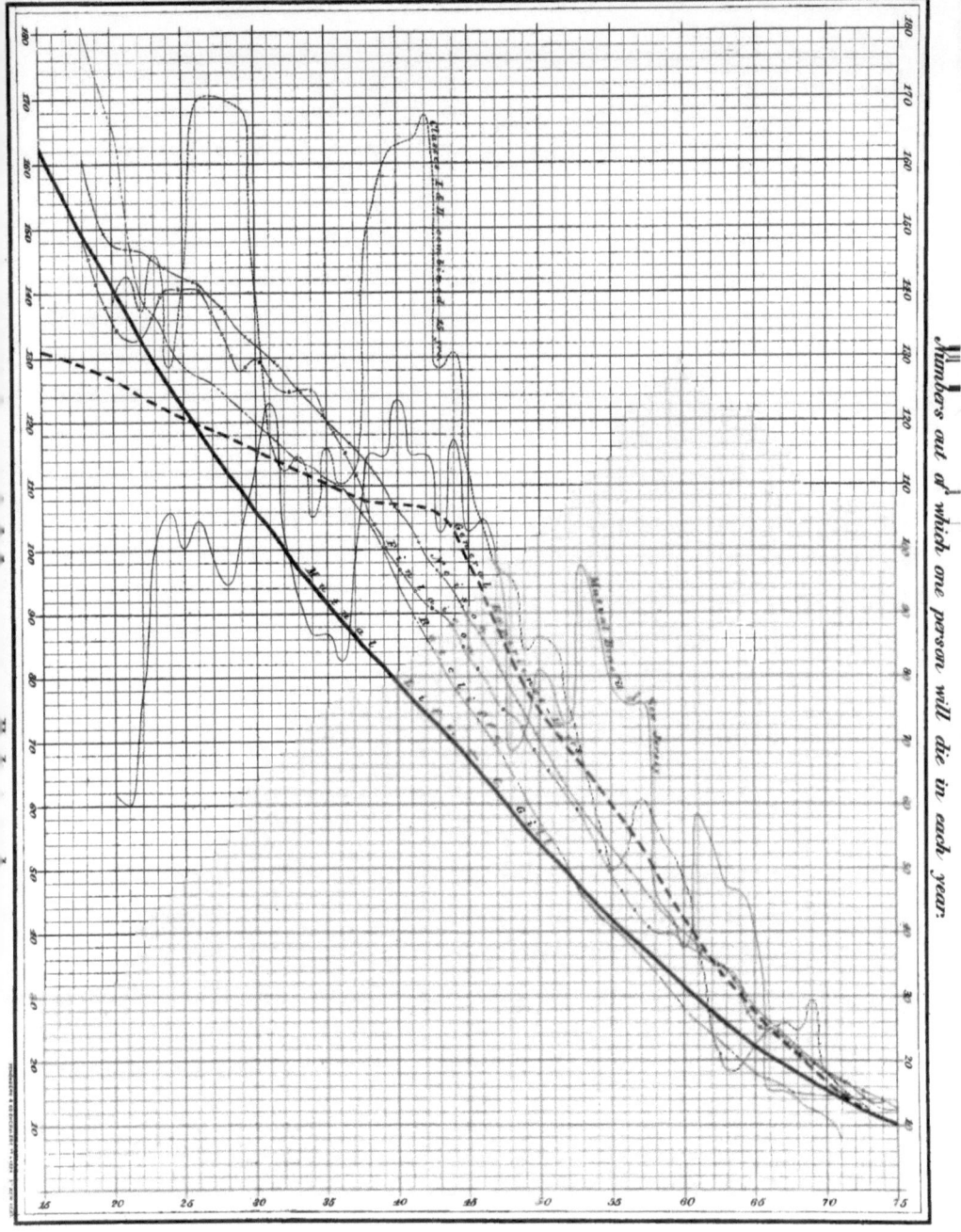

Ages.

EXPECTATION OF LIFE.

Perhaps the most interesting results of Table VII. are contained in the column headed "Expectation of Life," by which we may find for every age the *aftertime life*, or the number of years which, taking one person with another, we may expect to live. By means of the following table we may compare these numbers from our own Tables, with those according to some of the more celebrated English Tables of Mortality.

TABLE X.

EXPECTATION OF LIFE ACCORDING TO DIFFERENT TABLES OF MORTALITY.

Ages.	Mut. Life Office, C. Gill.	Mut. Life Experience, 15 years.	Eagle Experience, adjusted.	Actuaries' adjusted.	Carlisle.	Equitable Experience.	Amicable Experience.	Farr's English Life. No. 1.	Farr's English Life. No. 2.	English Friendly Societies. Ratcliffe, R. T. & C.	English Friendly Societies. Neison, R. T. & C. Main.	Economic Experience.	Massachusetts, 1855, Elliott.	Ages.
20	40.16	42.75	38.45	41.49	41.46	41.06	....	39.88	39.99	40.92	43.77	41.40	39.9	20
30	33.13	36.00	32.18	34.43	34.34	33.98	33.68	33.13	33.31	33.70	36.61	34.82	34.0	30
40	26.33	28.94	25.71	27.28	27.61	27.40	25.94	26.57	26.43	26.41	29.33	27.20	27.9	40
50	19.74	21.56	19.40	20.18	21.11	20.83	18.99	20.03	19.87	19.40	22.19	19.96	21.3	50
60	13.65	14.55	13.56	13.77	14.34	15.06	12.88	13.59	13.60	13.29	15.69	13.83	15.0	60
70	8.54	8.64	8.55	8.54	9.18	9.84	8.11	8.52	8.55	9.09	10.21	9.23	9.4	70

We here find that our Adjusted Experience gives a higher Expectation of life at all ages, than the Company's theoretical table, and also higher than any English table below the age of 70, except the "Friendly Societies" according to Neison, which is uniformly higher at all ages. At and above the age of 70, the Expectation by several English tables is higher than that shown by our own Experience.

COMPARATIVE MORTALITY IN ENGLAND AND IN THE NORTHERN UNITED STATES.

In a Report upon the Experience in 1851, Mr. Gill made a comparison of the actual rate of mortality among members of this Company residing in the Northern States, with that according to the experience of English Companies. I have extended that comparison so as to include our present results for fifteen years, together with the rate of mortality amongst the members of the Mutual Benefit Life Insurance Company of Newark, for twelve years, as published in their last Annual Report. We may thus compare the relative mortality among assured lives in this country and in England, at different ages.

TABLE IX.

COMPARISON OF THE ANNUAL RATE OF MORTALITY IN ENGLAND AND IN THE NORTHERN UNITED STATES.

	ENGLISH COMPANIES.		MUTUAL LIFE INSURANCE COMPANY OF N. Y.				"Mutual Benefit" Experience, 12 years.	N. Y. State Census, 1855.
	First year of Assurance.	Total Experience to 1893.	Classes I. and II. combined.		Class I. alone.	Whole Company.		
			8 years.	15 years.	15 years.	15 years.		
	A	B	C	D	E	F	G	H
15–25	....	....	....	.6838	.68	1.10	1.3363	.80
25–35	.5844	.7910	.7433	.8182	.73	.94	.9652	.77
35–45	.8872	1.1002	.8533	.8059	.76	.91	1.0027	1.04
45–55	1.3181	1.6140	1.2512	1.1783	1.16	1.28	1.2372	1.47
55–65	2.6755	2.9433	2.8011	2.7298	2.79	2.55	1.8544	2.10
65–75	3.4060	5.1769	8.9802	4.5252	3.85	4.34	4.9327	4.08

The first column (A) contains the annual rate of mortality among members of English Companies during their first year of assurance, or when the effect of selection was greatest. Column B contains the annual rate of mortality among members of the same Companies *after* their first year, or when the effect of selection is supposed to have diminished. Co lumns C, D, E, and F show the annual rate of mortality among members of this Company according to Experience; while column G shows the rate amongst all the members of the "Mutual Benefit" for twelve years. Column H contains the rate of mortality which I have deduced from the last Census of the State of New-York, but the Report itself is so badly arranged, at least in regard to mortality statistics, that I place no reliance upon the numbers in this column.

Theoretically, the rate of mortality among members of the American Companies should be greater than that shown by column A, but somewhat less than that of column B. We find, however, the rates shown by columns D and F are greater below the age of 35 than those in column B, while above that age they are somewhat smaller, and also that the rates shown in column E, for which alone our Table of Mortality was strictly intended, are *less at all* ages than that in column B, while for some ages they are even less than those shown by column A. The Experience of the "Mutual Benefit" also shows an unusual degree of mortality at younger ages, while at the middle and older ages the rates are somewhat less than those in column B.

From this we may see that the fear expressed by Mr. Gill, in the Report referred to, that the mortality in this country above the age of 55 would prove to be greater than that obtaining among similar classes in England, is not justified by the results of more extended Experience. On the contrary, the fear now seems to be that the mortality at younger ages may be greater than that anticipated, as we have already seen.

General Observations on the Results of the Company's Experience

The very favorable results in the Experience of this Company may be attributed to two principal causes, namely, the influence of *selection*, by which persons in sound health only, are admitted as members of the Company, and the fact that among these members are to be found so many *married* men, or heads of families.

The value of selection in this Company has not yet been ascertained. It has been found in England, however, that the value of life among persons selected with the greatest care, although at first greater than, yet gradually approximates to, the value among similar classes taken from the community at large. Whatever benefit we may have derived from judicious selection should not be considered as clear profit, but should be *set aside* in order to meet that *depreciation* in the value of life, which, in process of time, must be expected among members of long standing. In other words, although the deaths heretofore have been fewer in number than those predicted by standard Tables of Mortality, we should be prepared for the contingency, when present members become older, of having at some future time, *an Experience just the reverse of the present*.

The favorable influence of marriage upon the value of life has been long conceded, but has never been *numerically measured*, I believe, until very recently, when Dr. William Farr, F.R.S., read a paper before the British Association for the Advancement of Social Science, on the "Influence of Marriage upon the French People." Some of his results have been arranged in the following Table.

COMPARATIVE MORTALITY AMONG THE MARRIED AND SINGLE IN FRANCE, 1851.

Ages.	ANNUAL MORTALITY AMONG EACH 10,000 PERSONS LIVING.				Number of deaths among Single, corresponding to each 100 among the married	
	Husbands.	Bachelors.	Wives.	Spinsters.	Bachelors.	Spinsters.
Under 20	293	67	....	71	23	....
20–30	65	113	93	82	174	88
30–40	71	124	91	103	170	113
40–50	103	177	100	138	172	138
50–60	183	295	163	235	161	144
60–70	354	499	354	498	141	141

By this Table we observe that the mortality among husbands at the younger ages, is excessively high ; while the annual mortality among bachelors above the age of twenty is from 74 to 41 per cent greater than that among husbands.

May not this hold good, to a greater or lesser extent, in the United States ?

The very large number of *lapses* (other than by death or expiration) which, in this Company, is much greater in proportion, than among the English Companies, no doubt also exerts a great influence upon the foregoing results. Should these *lapses* in future materially decrease, we may expect an *increase* in the rate of mortality.

Before going further, it may be well to remark that the Table of Mortality now used by the Company, and upon which all rates of premium etc. are based, was constructed by your former Actuary, the late Prof. GILL, in a manner fully described by him in his introduction to "Assurance

Tables." Mr. GILL submitted his plan to some of the most experienced Actuaries in England, who gave it their unqualified approval, and no doubt, it was the best table for this country which could have been framed from information then obtainable. It is, however, entirely arbitrary, as far as regards the value of life in the United States, being a *mere digest* of the results of English observations. It is beautifully graduated, and reflects great credit upon the skill of its author. We have already seen that its predictions have been more than sufficient to cover the results of actual practice. Mr. GILL remarks, at the end of the description referred to above: " It is believed that this Table gives a more accurate representation of the value of the class of assured lives in *England,* than any other now extant. It will of course require to be modified for the United States, whenever *elements sufficiently reliable* can be procured." We can not rely upon the results of any Federal or State census in this country, for the purposes of Life Insurance, and besides it is very doubtful whether a Table of Mortality deduced from observations made upon a miscellaneous community, of men, women, and children, will ever represent with entire satisfaction, the value of life amongst *assured lives,* who are in many respects a *peculiar class.* Hence for the purpose of modifying or correcting our own Table of Mortality, *elements sufficiently reliable* can only be obtained from the Experience of our own or similar Life Insurance Companies.

For this reason, I have bestowed great care, and no small labor, in deducing from this Company's Experience, results which are as accurate, complete, and reliable as possible ; confident that if such observations are continued, we will soon have the requisite data for framing a reliable *American* Table of Mortality, and which will be an accurate representation of the relative value of life amongst the class of assured lives, at the different ages. The importance to this Company of such a table cannot be too

highly estimated, as affording the only means by which the scale of premiums can be equitably adjusted, or by which the present value of the
Company's contingent resources and liabilities, in a financial statement, may
be correctly ascertained.   Such a table, in fact, being absolutely essential
for the proper solution of all questions depending upon the duration of
human life.

At the present time, it may be safely said, that the comparatively
limited Experience of this Company, even when the very large number of
lives exposed to mortality is considered, will scarcely furnish results upon
which we may place implicit reliance—at least, not sufficient to justify
any change in the present rates of premium.   At the same time, however,
confirmed as they are by those of the "Mutual Benefit," our present results
of Experience prove that the Company's theoretical Table of Mortality
does not fairly represent the *comparative value* of assured lives *at different
ages*, in this country.   And consequently that our rates of premium are not
perfectly adjusted, being at some ages *too low*, and at others *too high* for the
risks which they are intended to cover.   Should these present results be
confirmed by future Experience *sufficiently extended*, a modification of our
table rates of premium will no doubt be necessary.   In the mean time, I
would respectfully suggest that any injustice which has been done to present members, by reason of the unequal graduation of premiums, may be
obviated, at least in part, by introducing results of Experience in such a
manner as to modify the *apportionment of each future dividend*, thus making
our system of reversionary dividends the *fly-wheel* or *governor* of the vast
machinery of Life Insurance.

The fact of charging at any age, comparative rates of premium slightly
too high or *too low*, is of but little consequence in a *Mutual* Company,
provided we have the means of making a just *compensation* to the original

contributors. The *amount* of such excess or deficiency in the rates of premium, can only be determined by tables based on actual Experience; while the *compensation* itself may be effected, as we have already seen, by a slight modification in the future apportionments of reversionary dividends.

Respectfully submitted to the Board of Trustees, by

SHEPPARD HOMANS,

Actuary.

NEW-YORK, *October 25th*, 1858.